my suicide note

I must have been pissed/or pissed off when i scribbled that signature, down below!

my suicide note

my suicide note

by
zak ferguson

my suicide note

I am dead, that or I am dying. I have been dying ever since I awoke fully, only to find I had been

my suicide note

introduced into this fucked up world. We are meant to die. Death is *of course* the most natural

my suicide note

part of existence. We are introduced to fail, suffer, and fight ourselves.

my suicide note

I am fed up.

I am knackered.

I am so, so, alone.

I am not free.

my suicide note

I am encumbered by so much. I try and I fail.

my suicide note

Still, at least my suicide note is going to be a book that will sell merely a few copies and have the reader

my suicide note

concerned about my mental health. Guess what? You are too late.

my suicide note

I am already dead. You just didn't know it.

my suicide note

SOCIAL MEDIA MELTDOWNS RESULT IN FAMOUS QUOTES FOR LATER USE & ABUSE.

my suicide note

my suicide note

my suicide note

I WANT TO EXPRESS. I WANT TO BE SETTLED. I WANT TO SHARE IN MOMENTS & I NEVER GET THEM.

my suicide note

my suicide note

I'M VERY DOWN. PLEASE HELP ME BACK UP. MIND MY PALMS, THEY'RE STICKY.

my suicide note

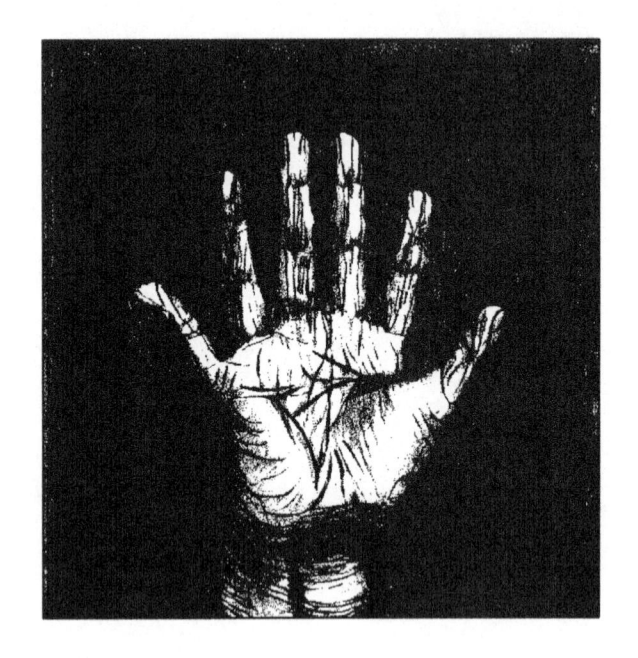

my suicide note

THE DREAM ME HAS DESTROYED THE REAL ME. DOES THIS MEAN THAT THE DREAM ME, IS THE ME I HAVE ALWAYS WANTED TO BE?

my suicide note

my suicide note

WE SLEEP ALL THE TIME BECAUSE WE WISH TO DIE. BUT WE ARE STILL SCARED OF DEATH. THE SLEEP IS NICE, THE DEATH, NOT SO MUCH.

my suicide note

my suicide note

CONCRETE PILLOWS ARE ONLY COMFORTABLE WHEN YOU ARE USED TO NO PILLOWS OR PILLOWS MADE OF LIME.

my suicide note

my suicide note

WE HAVE A SOCIAL MEDIA PLATFORM, LIKE THIS ONE*, SO WE CAN SEND OUT BOLD STATEMENTS & REFLECTIONS. ONLY FOR THEM TO DISSOLVE.

*Referring to Facebook.

my suicide note

my suicide note

PROSE POETRY/POETRY/

SOCIAL MEDIA SOAP-BOXER-Y IS MERE UNLIMITED SCROLLS OF DIGITAL CHAFF & INFECTED THOUGHT.

my suicide note

my suicide note

I AM DUMBFOUNDED BY YOUR DUMB FACES, PETULANTLY STRETCHED AT THE ABSURDITY OF MY WORKFLOW.

my suicide note

my suicide note

I HAVE NO TIME TO CHANGE/SHAPE/HELP YOU CREATE YOUR WEIRD EGO. LEARN TO ACCEPT OR DIE!

my suicide note

my suicide note

A BULLY IS A MAN WITH SO LITTLE GOING FOR HIMSELF HE MUST EXPRESS BY VIOLENCE, THROUGH WORDS AND DISGUSTING FISTS.

my suicide note

my suicide note

MY MOTHER HAD A HABIT OF ZIPPING ME UP IN THINGS. MY COCK'S FORESKIN & MY BOTTOM LIP. IT WAS A WEIRD METHOD OF DISPLAYING MOTHERLY LOVE.

my suicide note

my suicide note

I RETCHED INTO A MAN'S BUTT CHEEKS & HE REPLIED WITH A FART FLECKED WITH MY VOMIT. IT WAS NOT SEXY. IT WAS PERVERTED.

my suicide note

my suicide note

I NEVER EXPLORED MY SEXUALITY IN THE WAY MY MOTHER FEARED FOR ME. I HATE NEVER GETTING SUCH OPPORTUNITIES.

my suicide note

my suicide note

I CHOSE LONELINESS LIKE SHERLOCK HOLMES CHOSE OPIUM & WATSON'S HOMOSEXUAL COATS & HATS & CANES & POOR CHOICE OF WIVES & LOVERS.

my suicide note

my suicide note

I WON A BOX OF CHOCOLATES, FOR BEING A FILM ENCYCLOPAEDIA WHEN I WAS LESS GREEDY & SKINNIER. A DEEP REGET. AS I AM NOW HUNGRY.

my suicide note

my suicide note

I AM NOT A WRITER. I AM NOT AN EXPERIMENTER. I AM A VILE WASTE OF SPACE. I AM WHAT THE EGO MADE ME/WHAT IT DIDN'T MAKE ME. A GOD.

my suicide note

my suicide note

I ASK FOR BLURBS BECAUSE I ADORE THE FUTILITY OF THEM. I ADMIRE THE ARTISTS/WRITERS WHILST I LOATHE THE WORK, I EXPECT THEM TO "PRAISE".

my suicide note

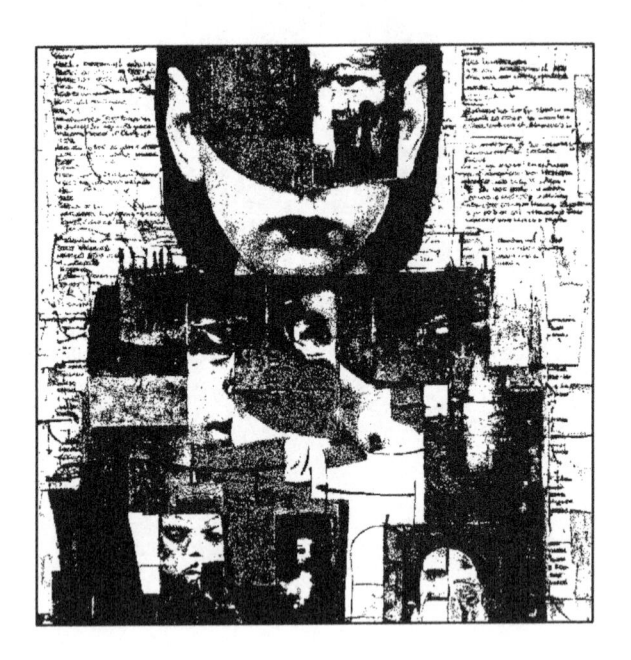

my suicide note

I LISTEN! I REALLY LISTEN, TO WHAT YOU SAY & PUT OUT. DO I EXPECT MUCH IN RETURN? YES. ONE EARLOBE ON A SILVER PLATTER...PLEASE.

my suicide note

my suicide note

KENJI SIRATORI HAS CREATED A NEW METHOD OF EXPRESSION. SOCIAL MEDIA PROJECTED QUOTES TO LIVE & CRY BY.

my suicide note

my suicide note

JOIN THE CULT OF KENJI BECAUSE HE DOES NOT BELIEVE IT IS A CULT, BUT A WAY OF TRANS-HUMANISING YOUR PATHETIC WORDS.

my suicide note

my suicide note

POSTING SONG LYRICS ON THIS DIGITAL DEVICE, IS COOL & ALL THAT, BUT WHY CAN'T YOU JUST MAKE UP YOUR OWN?

my suicide note

my suicide note

BEING CALLED WEIRD BY MY PEERS & FRIENDS MEANS MORE TO ME THAN YOU COULD EVER KNOW. IT IS RECOGNITION OF MY INDIVIDUALITY.

my suicide note

my suicide note

INDIE ARTISTS MAKE NO MONEY. WE ASK FOR LITTLE & WHEN WE DO, OTHER INDIE ARTISTS MOCK US. WHAT IS WRONG WITH YOU "PEOPLE".

my suicide note

my suicide note

I ASK FOR ANSWERS & READ THE WORD "ANSWER" AS AN-SWERVES.

my suicide note

my suicide note

SOCIAL MEDIA MELTDOWNS AS TRANSLATED BY THE NORMIES. IT IS NOT A MELTDOWN; IT IS EXPRESSION & REBELLION.

my suicide note

my suicide note

I WAS DUMPED ONCE BECAUSE SHE DIDN'T WANT ME BECAUSE SHE HAD HER OWN MENTAL HEALTH ISSUES, THEN DATED AN ABUSER. KARMA-CHAMELEON?

my suicide note

my suicide note

TAPED TO A CHAIR/TAPE-GAGGED, UNTIL BLACK EYED PEAS CHANGED THE COURSE OF MY FUTURE HISTORY.

my suicide note

my suicide note

IF DAVID ATTEN-BOI-ER NARRATED MY LIFE, HE'D SMASH THE MICROPHONE & PAY FOR MY PERSONAL EXECUTION.

my suicide note

my suicide note

I PREFERRED RICHARD ATTENBOROUGH TO LITTLE BROTHER, DAVID. WHY? BECAUSE HE WAS FAR MORE TALENTED, THAT'S WHY!

my suicide note

my suicide note

SWEAT DRENCHED PRESS WAS A FAILURE FROM THE START. THE REASON FOR SAID FAILURE WAS IT WAS NECESSARY FOR THE PRESS - YOU HEAR ME?

my suicide note

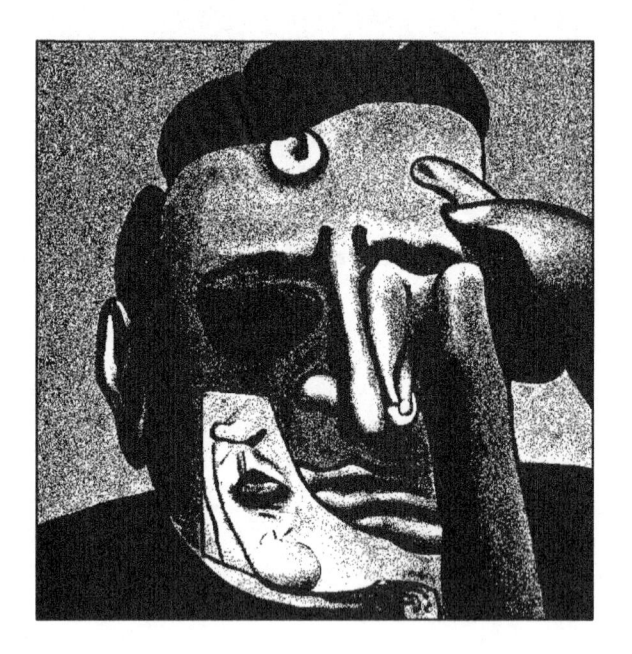

my suicide note

ARTISTS & THEIR BAD HABITS ARE NOT FOR ME, SO FUCK OFF WITH YOUR MANIA AND BS! I HAVE BETTER HEADS TO CHOP OFF AND FERMENT.

my suicide note

my suicide note

FACEBOOK IS THREATENING ME AGAIN OVER THE WORD FUCK & OFF AND FERMENTATION, IN RELATION TO CHOPPING OFF HEADS. CUNTS.

my suicide note

my suicide note

WORDS THAT WILL OFFEND, TRIGGER & UPSET FACEBOOK - SELF-EXPRESSION.

my suicide note

my suicide note

I PLAYED KNOCK-KNOCK-GINGER ON A STREET THAT WAS CORDONED OFF/WHERE HOUSES WERE LEFT UNOCCUPIED. IT WAS A THRILL. ALSO, I WAS A WIMP.

my suicide note

my suicide note

I WAS A SKINNY BOI BEFORE I WAS A FAT BOY, & THEN I WAS AN EVEN SKINNIER BOYI-BUOY-BOY, BEFORE I AM THE FAT BASTARD I AM NOW.

my suicide note

my suicide note

DON'T BE SCARED OF THESE WORDS.

my suicide note

THIS ISNT WILD/ CONCERNING.

my suicide note

THIS ISN'T INSANITY UNLEASHED.

my suicide note

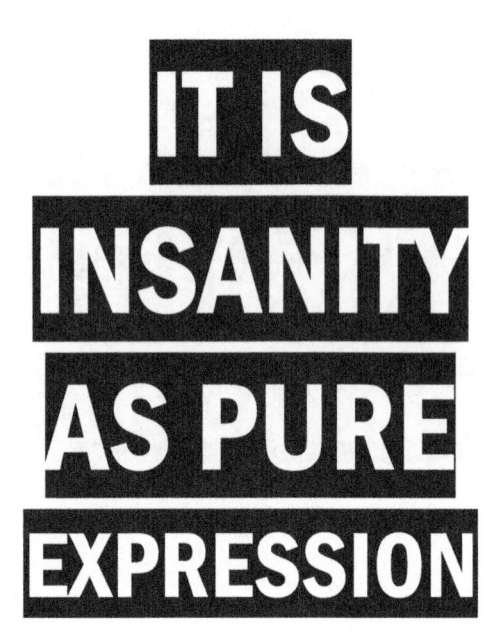

IT IS
INSANITY
AS PURE
EXPRESSION

my suicide note

I AM
NO MORE
NO LESS

my suicide note

I am a scab that has long been forgotten.

I am that scab you picked at and got scolded for irritating.

I am the scab that once metastasized and sold a cottage in Belgium.

I am the scarab that faked being a barnacle on the elbow of Long John Dipshit.

I am that scab that left you worried that it might be signs of something worse... something that begins with the dreaded C.

I am the scab of scabs, small, rotten, perhaps innocuous when left to its own devices outside of all the other shit you have going on with your body.

I am the scab that is an epicentre to so many unexpressed feelings you have bottled up.

I am expressing. Fear not.

I fear nothing.

Nor should you.

You used to sing to your scabs.

What? You don't remember?

I am trying to protect you.

I am that scab.

I am Dali reborn as a scab.

my suicide note

my suicide note

I am Bacon reborn as a mole, beneath the testicles of a reborn lover.

I am the lover reborn as part of the hive mind of the first scab to be picked and kept in a safe place, to grow old and retire in the bottom of Davy Jones's locker.

He forgot his padlock code.

Tentacles are slippery.

I am scabrous.

I am scabs.

Loads of them.

All with a hive mind.

Forcing you to admit defeat in the face of all the talent that comes before you.

I am a scab that has recently been found on a part of your body that you had yet to realise had important capillaries inflaming – screaming, wriggling, wiggling, grinding, pulsating, notifying you of the infection ready to blow up your stupid little world.

I am the picked scab.

I am the scar from such a scab.

I am a scab in both senses, the ultra-sense and the nonsense.

I am a writer by trade, meaning I am on the dole.

my suicide note

my suicide note

I am healing your wounds by applying my own warped methodology.

I am your puckered anus calling for a time out.

I am Medusa posing in a compact mirror, on a tram on my way to work, trying to catch any old fools eye, so once I have turned him into stone – or whatever passes for cement this day and age - my work day is complete.

I am the cotton bud shoved into your rearend when you were four, and you couldn't cope with the feeling of me being twisted, wiggled, up into your poo-pipe, by your demented mother, most likely unaware that this can produce phantom orgasms at such an age- searching for worms, that themselves were shocked by a solid cue-tip lodged into their secret abode. Casa Anushole.

I am the exploded viscera from all the wars fought without any input from your nation, and still, I want you to feel guilty.

I am the FBI agent assigned to tail Donald Trump who is going out on the campaign trails, once again, with little to no change to his personality, and no matter how often I tail him on his various whacko-trails, he doesn't show any form of fear.

I am tomato ketchup mixed with mustard on a corndog, cooling under the breeze that has made a long trip of the coldest of climes, under the fading light of mid-afternoon, the sky concluding earlier than it has done before.

my suicide note

If we slept with Rogue from the X-Men comics, would she suck us into non-existence?

We have no powers here.

We have no fuel here.

Rogue has a bodacious booty on her, displaying the artists perverted natures.

Posing in photos with your weighty chunky rings, that you so love, and have kept nestled in a most specific box – the box itself extremely kitschy - until somebody rushes into your makeup room and announces, "Today is the day!" – and you know what they mean; they mean photoshoot time with Vogue – and you pull this gaudy medium-sized, 26 ½ x 18.5 jewellery box from your special drawer – the drawer that you need ten keys to unlock. These variously sized and bejewelled rings are the symbols of success and attainment – as you popped them on you felt real, realer than real, for a change - they are built to emphasize the hands you do or do not have, and the masculinity some people seem to believe hands convey – odd, you humans - and when these photos are published, and not viewed in print, as they were intended, but copied, screen-shot, passed from one corruptible little soul to the next willing and already infected and malevolent fucker, the photos are blurry, its overall intention, in all its high-resolution, is messed up, passed on and on, until the image that represents whatever narrative these tools are passing off as "real" becomes the only story and only essence to said photographs; and

my suicide note

you lose out on a film role with Disney because your finger-jewels look like you are smoking. Nothing as extreme as a joint or acid-reefer, but a normal casual cigarette. Fuck this world. Fuck Dizz-Knee. Fuck the pathetic weasels that want to destroy you for the sake of annihilation.

No more.

No less.

No less, with potential for more.

So much more.

Ancient aliens do not exist – why? – because they do not subscribe to this doctrine the religions and the scientists have created for us – which is? – the concept of time – they do not play in that field – the fuck with it.

Scrolling through news articles and big, brash, bold headlines I cannot help but weave the now into the work – it might age it, later in life, but that in many ways documents the times we be living in, dear fellow scribblers of nonsense.

We are on the coffin trail.

The hunted are now hunters.

Tracking fictive forms.

Howling our own versions of long-ago wolves-howls that had been cut off mid-howl – forever silenced by the sharpest end of an axe. Incapacitated by the

my suicide note

blunt end, crushing their skulls inward, imploding their brains from out of their arrow tipped ears.

The sharpest end of the axe isn't the blade, but the man who wields it.

Unlimited tags and too much control over other people's social media fates.

Stop.

Slow down.

my suicide note

A mountain is only a mountain when it is built out of crashed landed UFO parts and a miscellany of variously melted/liquefied materials.

Spying on its continual development is a strange, masked man called Petey.

Petey is in a hazmat suit, fitted with various holes, stitched over with different medals, one's that had been butchered by a onehanded blacksmith, and scorched from the fires of someplace called Heaven, others fitted with dials and complicated mechanical gizmos to channel the chemicals that kept him stuck between the ages of one thousand and fifty and one thousand and fifty-one.

He had a strange relationship with time.

He once worked in the field of string theory and got kicked out because he ended up showing up the heads of department with his presentation using rope and opining that string was nonsense and rope was indeed sacred.

Neurons stretched out from his brain as ectoplasmic materials and hardened within the enclosed area that sealed his head into his adapted headgear/helmet/gasmask - that webbed themselves out — thick vines of essence - fighting against the various neurological diseases fighting to end his long thousand-year life.

Petey had often been mistaken as a gas-masked creature looking through a telescope implanted into his face, when that was Bracken, the local quack who based his look on Petey, having obsessed since he was a child of cosplaying Petey.

Petey was a walking (non-verbal, yet in essence totally verbal) and talking myth, that was merely made mythic because he disappeared off and on, between local visitors admiring his handywork/mountain project. And, considering the people of this rotten world, who genetically have been fucked by those of the year 2000 and onwards, by low attention spans and forgetfulness, these new world examples of homo sapiens have little to no attention spans, that if he left the local area and returned an hour later, the myth inside related to him would still hit them as hard as the return of Hey-Zeus himself.

Petey was made real and photographable, but that didn't stop Bracken from idealising him to the point he started going to black market flesh-alternators and having himself adapted, in as best a replication as they could (legally, as Petey was known for suing people for plagiarism over his look) to that of Petey's steampunk gone to seed aesthetic.

But Bracken would never be the… thing that Petey was, as he sadly came from the same generation as those I have just ridiculed.

He wasn't the real McCoy in relation to his looks and intentions, that and the need for the weird metallic structures embedded and stitched into his Frankensteinian-monster face.

Petey breathed chemicals, exhaled pure and unique air, he started selling it off to the highest bidder, all so he could use the finance to continue digging up long lost UFO artefacts and melting them/reshaping them to fit his mountain project.

Petey lived in an old FUF-5000XD depot station, one he dug up from beneath the crust of what was once known as Scot 'Lund.

It was shaped like a skull – but he didn't like it, so kept building extra extensions from various other fighter-pilots and space-stations and refuelling posts.

He preferred the look of a bird in flight.

Then once he got bored of an avian skull that might have some simian DNA in there, he overhauled it all and just outright purchased a TUNDRA-NO-UNDRA deep sleep foetus colony ship, minus the foetuses. This had a long centre-prong – the height of the once proud EMPIRE STATE OF NO NATION BUILDING, with of course Petey specific extensions.

The centre fuselage was converted to keep his latest invention, The Craggle-Grug-Grub-ErZ515s as a "sleeping" quarter.

He designed it like he had designed a suite for the ex-fighters who battled for war for Treshranana-Shultz on the grand Mary Celestial CrestFallen-Wing-DRZR00978-craft, that later, like most Petey designs spread out into becoming crafts that when

my suicide note

terraformed created a station, that then was expanded into a living planet.

A living planet with the personality of Kenneth Williams, one of histories most respected and most versatile actor in all human history.

(Minor note, there existed only Kenneth Williams compilation videos lasered onto huge, pond-sized discs and Steven Seagal compilation videos onto little Mem sticks, and we all know who out of the wo is more a worthy actor than the other.)

my suicide note

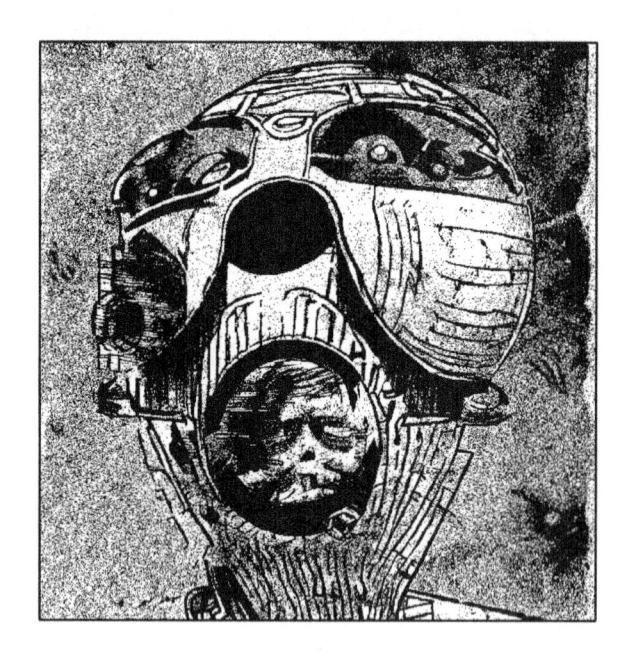

my suicide note

my suicide note

my suicide note

I am not a science fiction writer.

I am not a contemporary writer.

I am nothing.

I am a shell.

Put me up to your ear, and tell the world what you believe you hear, compared to what you can hear.

It is oblivion.

my suicide note

my suicide note

my suicide note

WORDS ARE NO LONGER WORDS.

THEY ARE EMBLEMS

my suicide note

Andrew McMaughty would say he was like any other teenager.

In our current era not that many teenagers could claim that/nor wouldn't wish to be seen like the majority.

Being part of the crowd was so 1970.

The current era of youths wants to stand out in all their uniqueness.

Their identity as approved by the masses - usually via social media.

Andrew didn't have too much awarenesses outside of himself, whilst not being all that aware of himself.

He was aware but not aware to the heightened degrees teenagers are now.

He liked listening to music - the most chart topping the song is the better.

He liked sports.

He loved video games.

What made Andrew stand out was that he didn't think himself any different from the rest.

He wasn't special.

He wasn't unique.

He wasn't conflicted and confused.

He just got on with things.

my suicide note

Now, many might say he was a cookie-cutter/carbon copy of the blandest of personalities, but in a world full of too much personality, he was a breath of fresh fucking air.

He wasn't bent over double in insecurity and never questioned his sexuality nor his personality.

He was just Andrew.

He got on with everything in a breezy, unhurried, but decidedly clear manner.

He got on well with both sexes.

He got on with those that didn't wish to be gendered.

He was, in his opinion, alright.

He was 17 years of age.

He was studying to be an electrician at College.

He secured himself an apprenticeship with a local plumbing empire.

He was happy with that.

He had money unlike most of his college and long-lasting school friends.

He did though once get obsessive over something.

This is Andrew's obsession:

my suicide note

A MILITARY MAN FEATURED IN AN ADVERT.

my suicide note

I was watching TV like most kids my age do.

I was and wasn't.

I was looking from phone to television.

The phone was on silent, so I wasn't that heavily invested in the usual things people gush over.

The phone passes the time between ad breaks and whatever repeat of some cringe American sitcom is screaming the canner laughter at us not so stupid Brits to laugh along with.

An ad popped up with a pomp who was in a corduroy waist coat.

My attention was tractor-beamed onto him.

My phone became weightless and could have broken the laws of gravity and lifted itself from my phone and made off and I wouldn't have cared or been aware of such a decreet exit.

This pomp, this man of the aristocracy was promoting his charity.

Something about water.

Don't ask me what it was but his voice gripped me.

I looked into his eyes as if he were appealing to me, and me alone.

I noticed he had placed himself in front of a very lacking bookshelf.

my suicide note

The spines of all his books were mostly of a hardcover variety with that glossy dust jacket glint, reflecting the light they had projecting onto him for the interview.

I leaned in, but before I could note some of the titles the ad flicked through its mirage of footage of black dying babies and a heavily accented African doctor holding his palm out, as if unveiling some terrible prize that can be won on an old gameshow, telling the world that antibiotics could save these dying black babies.

The old pomp's voice was still narrating, his voice deep, baritone, pitched at a monotone – at an even level throughout.

Before the end of the ad, the 5 second obligatory thank you's, I scanned the bookshelves.

Still, I couldn't pick out any decipherable name.

There was one big chunky book with a soldier, with a beret on his head, the colour of his red hat stark against the military greens and browns of his uniform that I could process in those mere seconds afforded.

The glossy dustjacket design was also patterned with military colours and chameleon shapes, but the dust jacket was a different hue of the militia pattern of the officer's own uniform, perhaps deliberately done so they did not to merge into one splodge.

The ad ended.

I was straight onto my iPhone.

I looked it up, found it, after various ridiculous Google search results, and I watched it, OVER AND OVER, AGAIN.

I slowed it down.

I went frame by frame.

my suicide note

I created a history for this pomp.

Again, I went frame by frame.

I could easily have searched who this man was, but I was overtaken by this urge to create a new personality from this… obsession.

He was there for me to idealise and construct.

To criticise. To embellish.

The bookshelves and their initial focus and importance to my intrigue died out, as a new obsession took hold.

This man's jowls were strange.

He looked rubbery, and unreal, like a creation from Kazuhiro Tsuji.

Frame by frame, I went through it.

I purchased an app that highlighted stills and improved their quality.

It seemed to to fail.

Lagging and eventually being corrupted by the same pixelated glitch issue.

The picture quality kept separating, colours and resolution fracturing into pixelated data and his voice intruded on the still images of these digital codes.

This obsession merely altered in specific spots, fragments of the overall piece I had framed for myself.

New obsessions were born that day… from that damned advert/promotional/self-entitled pomp charity piece.

my suicide note

I am now a benefit bum, unable to work and wipe my own butt.

I have been corrupted.

By an aristocratic pomp.

my suicide note

This is my suicide note.

Fuck you.

Fuck all of you, that have hurt me so deeply that I have no other route to go buy total oblivion.

Your words have staying power.

Your attacks too.

I cannot cope under this pressure.

I feel the weight of all the Greek Gods on my shoulders, and they aren't there to put pressure on me, they think they are all having a laugh, not at my expense, but at the nature of human's toil.

It isn't a specific attack on me, I am not going to assign victimhood to myself, that just isn't fair, for those who have suffered real, truer trauma.

I feel my heart pump.

I sense the blood flow will soon come up against a blockage.

This is my suicide.

Knowing that my body wants to kill me and doing nothing to prevent that eventuality.

my suicide note

I have been haunted by visions of a young man cut in half. No penis. No buttocks. No left arm. No legs. No normal circuitry to keep him going – yet technology is striving to keep him alive, to suffer those phantom limb pains. I would just ask to be put to sleep.

He has a partner willing to care for him.

No future.

No penis penetration.

All of this technological advancement to save him, and they really should have asked, should they have even attempted to keep this literally halved person alive.

Mere tongue satisfaction.

Is that enough for him?

Does he get phantom cock throbs?

Does he cry at these pangs of sexual lust via a penis that is now, no more?

Five minutes ago, my head hurt.

Is it that roll-Up I had?

Has all these years without smoking tobacco insistently/consistently just slapped me with a miraculous brain clot, tumour, or brain-spasm?

Or the brain tumour I think poofs into existence with each paranoid thought.

my suicide note

I fear death.

So-fucking-much.

I like to think I am spiritual.

Some days more so than others.

I want the other world to make itself known.

I want to feel it.

I do not want the death part of it.

Transgressive author – but, never given the perk of being transgressive in life.

I want to say to so many, fuck you, you are one nasty looking cunt.

Do I get a hall pass when a certain majority feel the same way as I do?

Ha!

No!

Why?

Because, because, because...

The throbbing, strobing cock of a man call Osz!

No, not Ozz, or Oz. I meant to type Osz.

Because some person will *decide* to like *said* person all so they can *retaliate*.

The bigger the book the deadlier the weapon.

my suicide note

I want to take these words and use them as throwing stars... I imagine they would pack quite a punch unless they are of a NERF!-gun variety.

Soft bullets that expand over time, and you go to the doctor who diagnoses it as diabetic weight gain, even though you are not diabetic, yet you now are kid!

The bullets expand and when the time is right... BOOM! Gone. Dead.

Scattered to whatever winds are provided that day.

The gloss finish on that cover of a book, by Charles Brussard, whose title eludes me is overwhelming.

I am upset.

Angry.

Frustrated.

Agitated.

Ready to explode.

Nobody sees me or hears me.

I feel like I am going to just take the plunge and top myself...

I have tried before...

With insulin, but I hate how low blood sugars make me feel.

my suicide note

The second time I tried, our family dog Todd got his body underneath me and guided me back to shore. Fuck I miss that dog.

I am called all these names: abuser, harasser, bully, and all I do is give people one-hundred and ten percent of me. I do things on their behalf that no person should do and if there is an error in that execution, I *am* the *issue*.

Calling you *lazy* does not mean someone has *bullied* you.

It means you should think of what you have done to make someone call you *lazy*.

If by calling you lazy means I am a bully, a bully I shall be and am.

Do not send a book that you have zero clue as to the order of the images, and supposed corresponding prose, that you have created – sent in incremental parts, and expect a publisher to make your submission for you.

Do not think that they enjoyed the experience, where one artist involved says one thing, whereas the other says another, and between them they are bickering, and never actually highlighting the type of book that they want.

I am not psychic you twerps!

People fashion things to fit their moods and agendas and spitefulness.

my suicide note

I am honest.

I see things as straight forward and get aggrieved when people reveal that they do not want to follow the easiest and straight forward of paths, they want the messy uphill struggle and the downhill leg snapping result.

I am sapped of all energy.

Divas that don't deserve the diva stature they are exhibiting and using as a weapon.

I still apologise, for my own human frailties, and then, they pop off, make a scene, transform something relatively small into a nuclear blast of supposed intent on my behalf.

██████████████████████

██████████████████████

I want to at least be given a chance to bully, harass, or harm these people that fashion words to suit their moods and vile intents.

I want to break your legs and piss over you – not nice piss, nasty withheld urinary infection piss.

If I struck a match, you'd go up like a fucking Christmas tree, and your screams will resemble the popping of the pines.

I am a murderer at heart.

I visualise your deaths.

my suicide note

I map out how to get away with it… sadly, technology the world over isn't very helpful in a potential serial killer getting away with murder.

I need a car. An alibi. A friend who will never say anything about my deeds or their hand in said dead-related-deeds.

I want to cry these trapped aphanitic tears that are hurting my mind… but they won't come out, nor can come out, as they are like basalt shards. I could built an abstract mound out of thee tears, if only I could use a magma glue to keep these pieces together.

The bully calling others the bullier.

Coming out of his drugs den, the greasy, pungent wastrel known as Callum, sniffs the air, and decides, let me ruin somebody's day with my social media presence, my ugly mush, my projection to all I am.

Hearsay. Rumour. Words taken on as truth and there is no room for counterargument, or the truth of the matter.

I could destroy this wastrel, druggy, irregularly crazy, useless waste of human breath with a mere shrug… … … … and still I want to tear into his pathetic flesh. I want to break him down, and witness all that makes him who he is. A very simple minded, talented buffoon who loves confrontation.

I have butted head with so many people, no wonder I am dizzy and fatigued.

my suicide note

I put so much of myself into these things, no wonder I end up used and (the actually) abused.

I cannot stand self-victimisation, when you have lived your life as a victim, you witness these people jumping on social trends and acquiring words and hashtags, and implementing them in their pathetic life and bedsit landscape - but I am too scared to voice it and phrase it like that, because there is always one cunt like myself who will roll their eyes and mock them for identifying as an abused animal.

I wish we could throw people into a junk email and watch them battle within the confines of that folder – one side of you there is a sex-bot linking you up with all kinds of potential fraudster hacker shite, the other an email that starts with, **Dear Mrr. FERGUson** - you get no further – the weird hieroglyphs in the subject header enough to tell you, do not open it.

I imagine these virus-veined emails leaking and corrupting the bastard I had slammed into my junk email folder.

Can the digital virus take over where the viral-viral-attack and illness has been healed and fought against?

Can the digital virus kill you?

Yes, but it isn't via hackers and their odd links and sources of cookie-generated information – yes FB does listen to you, and no, they can never recommend the right things – it is the social media bully.

my suicide note

The person with so little to do with their lives they go in and make shit up.

And sadly, non-entities encourage other non-entities to rally and create an online lynch-mob – that people of little or large character pay attention.

Do not listen to them, they know not of what they make up, as that is how severe their minds are.

Social media is a disease.

This is my final book.

My final statement.

I do not want to be a writer anymore.

I do not want a social presence to uphold and keep alive.

I am tired.

So very tired.

This book is my suicide note.

It might be a long wait until I have the balls to go through with it.

my suicide note

my suicide note

Copyright 2024 ©
Zak Ferguson

Copyright 2024 ©
Sweat Drenched
Press

Cover art by
Zak Ferguson

my suicide note

This book or any portion thereof may not be reproduced or used in any manner whatsoever without the express written permission of the publisher or writer except for the use of brief quotations in a book review or article.

my suicide note

ISBN:
9798876257154

my suicide note

This is a work of fiction. Names and characters are the product of the authors imagination and any resemblances to actual persons, living or dead, is entirely coincidental.

All rights reserved.

my suicide note

my suicide note

ABOUT THE AUTHOR

He is dead.

He is dying.

Nobody will mourn him.

my suicide note